MW01538199

# IMPORTANT CONVERSATIONS THROUGH SHORT STORY STARTERS

*By Paris E. Moore*

*Cover drawing*
*and*
*illustrations by Lewis Tronson*
*E-mail: lewis.tronson@gmail.com*

All rights reserved. No part of this book may be reproduced or transmitted in any form or by any means, electronic or mechanical, including photocopying, recording, or by any information storage and retrieval system, without permission from the copyright owner.

This book was printed in the United States of America.
Copyright © 2019 Paris E. Moore
**ISBN:** 9798613970995
**Imprint:** Independently published

# INTRODUCTION

Being in ministry and working in the area of specials needs to support families for several years has allowed me to understand that the elements in these stories are shared by many people. Men and women. Hopefully we can open up dialogue, create safe places to talk, and maybe better understand each other.

 This book of short story starters lends itself to important conversation about indifference, strength, influence, power, and willpower to survive.

The purpose of these stories is to spark inter-generational conversations that discuss mutual respect, decision making, problem solving, personal accountability, anger management, feelings, and emotions in a way that can bring about understanding, support, and application. Hopefully this model encourages the strengthening of positive relationships and the building of healthy personal boundaries.

The hope is to be aware that everything we do, feel, think, and say is important. Everything we do, feel, think, and say not only dictates how we behave as individuals and impacts others. We can never know the true impact we have had on other people's lives until they tell us.

If our intent is to do something good and it turns out bad, the positive or negative result will still have happened. Every action has a reaction, every choice has a consequence, and every intent has an impact. None of us is perfect. The best we can do is the best we can do at the time. Either way (good or bad), we need to take responsibility for our part, learn the lesson, bring the wisdom forward, apply it to the present, move on in a safe way, and leave the trash behind!

These are big concepts for young or overwhelmed minds. That is why these important conversations through story starters is a great way for everyone to think out loud in a safe environment. Allow the characters to be the catalyst to express hurt feelings, regrets, love, sorrows, happiness, curiosity, accomplishments, and hope for tomorrow.

**Activity option:** At the end of each story, the participants could either rewrite the story from their own precative or share it verbally.

**Note**: Include in your conversation words like **forgiveness.**
What does it look like? Who needs to be forgiven and why?

## Determination
What is it? Who needs it and why?

## Pride
Is it good, bad, or no big deal? Give an example and explain your point.

## Power
What is it? Who needs it? Who should have it? Is it good or bad? Explain.

## Anger and Depression
Ho does anger or depression begin? Do they always happen together? Explain. Name some things that would help? Explain.
## Love
Does love look the same to all people in relationships?

## Empathy and Kindness
What do they mean? Are they important? Explain.


These are just a few suggestions. Let's get started.

# Pride and Joy

## Story #1

Mr. Pride, the owner of a circus, was in the jungle enjoying the sights and sounds when he saw an elephant he thought was special. He decided she was just what his circus needed. With no regard for her well-being, he arranged to capture her and make her the star attraction. So, he captured her and took her away from the things she loved in order to serve his purpose.

Mr. Pride was excited about the wonderful things to come, the crowds, the money, and all the places they would visit. Mr. Pride never once gave any thought to what the elephant might have to suffer in order to fulfill his needs. Mr. Pride decided to call her Joy because that is what he felt when he saw her. Mr. Pride was good to this elephant, or so he thought. He had her hosed down regularly for her bath. Joy did miss being able to take a bath in the river, toss dirt on her back or wallow in the mud whenever she took a notion. Even more, Joy missed taking walks through the jungle with her family and friends. Joy really was happiest right where Mr. Pride had found her.

Joy was curious about this new place and began walking around, but the people didn't understand. Sometimes Joy would accidently crush something important as she walked by or scared people when she was trying to exercise her legs by running in the area.

Mr. Pride was not being selfish intentionally, he merely had no need to see beyond his own needs. So, he didn't. Mr. Pride soon found that Joy kept walking away, but Joy could not be allowed to roam freely in her new environment. In an attempt to keep her safe and in control, Mr. Pride came up with what he thought was a marvelous idea. He hammered a strong spike into the ground. Then he attached a twenty-foot chain to it with a shackle attached to the opposite end and secured it around one of Joy's legs welding it shut.

Obviously, this created a problem for Joy. She was confined and whenever she tried to go in any direction beyond the twenty-foot chain, she was gripped with pain. Truth be told, Joy was not trying to leave. She was just curious about her new environment. Joy could not understand why Mr. Pride was being mean to her. Mr. Pride gave Joy the best care money could buy, but she was still unable to enjoy her captivity. Mr. Pride was feeling very good about the fact he never beat Joy the way other handlers did their elephants.

Well eventually, Mr. Pride got his way, but Joy's long captivity was taking its toll. Joy quit trying to do the very things that kept her healthy, strong, and happy. She didn't extend her trunk to the children in a playful manner like she used to do. And the walks she used to try to take when she wanted to stretch her legs stopped happening altogether. Instead of doing her own thinking, she began to do things only as she was told. This made Mr. Pride very happy. He was now feeling the effects of his power. He was in complete control of a life other than his own. The whole time Mr. Pride was smiling and bragging to the other handlers about his so-called accomplishment. Mr. Pride's victory was also Joy's defeat.

Joy made no more attempts to explore her surroundings. She lost her desire to look for tasty treats only her homeland could offer. After many failed attempts to investigate her new surroundings, Joy learned to stay in her place. Her will was broken. The physical chains that once held her in place were no longer necessary, so Mr. Pride removed them.

Joy only did things as she was commanded. She brought great happiness to the millions of people who were in her audiences. The people were struck with awe as they gazed upon this beautiful, strong, and massive creature doing the tricks just as they had been rehearsed. The audience members were committing every detail of this flawless performance to memory. Their plan was to tell their family and friends later.

Sadly, the wonder of this event escaped Joy. She was merely doing her job. There was no more to it than that! After all, her ability to make choices had been taken away from her. The people she was entertaining were there by their choice. They were enjoying her ability at their will, not hers.

Mr. Pride came to realize their relationship had changed. He needed Joy as much as she needed him. He had become dependent upon Joy to help him with things he could not do for himself. For example, tents could not be set up without Joy's help. Joy moved heavy objects with the greatest of ease. Without Joy, it would take the strength of several people to get the circus ready for visitors. By now Joy was well trained, and people came from all around to see her. The most amazing thing was Joy remained gentle enough to be around the audiences who loved her so much.

As you can imagine, Joy's frustration eventually gave way to the complacency that allowed her to merely exist in this limited surrounding. Joy never realized how much happiness she gave to others. She was simply enduring the pain and suffering Mr. Pride mistakenly thought was taking good care of her. From Mr. Pride's perspective, things were very good, but from Joy's perspective they were very bad. Together they did what they had to do to get to the next day.

The time finally came when Joy was getting old and the circus life was taking its toll. Mr. Pride wanted to do something nice for Joy, so he arranged to take her back to the place where he had captured her. Mr. Pride thought he was being kind by giving Joy her freedom.

Ordinarily this would have been a good thing, but Mr. Pride had not taken his previous actions into consideration. As quickly and abruptly as Joy was taken from her homeland years ago, she was returned to it. Only now her youth was gone. Nothing looked familiar. Joy had a hard time accepting this was happening again. With tears in her eyes, trying to understand what had taken place, Joy was stunned!

The every-day sights and sounds that once filled Joy's day with happiness and intrigue before Mr. Pride took her struck fear and anguish in her heart now that she was back, because freedom was no longer her source of security. Captivity was. Mr. Pride was oblivious to Joy's inner turmoil or the damage he caused her by inflicting his will on her year after year.

So, Mr. Pride left Joy there and told himself she would be back to her old self in no time. With that thought in mind, Mr. Pride said, "Good-bye," and made his journey home.

Many seasons came and left. Mr. Pride realized he missed his old friend. He missed her so much. He finally took a vacation and went to see how Joy was enjoying her freedom. Mr. Pride wondered if Joy had a family now. He wondered how hard it would be to find her now that she was free to go in any direction as far as her eyes could see. Mr. Pride so looked forward to seeing Joy run through the trees the way she did before he captured her.

Mr. Pride planned to begin his search down by her favorite watering hole, if he could remember its location. Oh, how Mr. Pride's eyes ached to see his old friend. Much to his surprise, he found Joy almost at once. There she was. She was free to do whatever she pleased, go wherever she wanted and in any direction without exception, no boundaries or pain. Yet, there she was standing not more than twenty feet away from where her freedom was supposed to begin.

**You can never know the true impact you have had on someone else's life until they share it with you. Everything else is speculation.**

1. Mr. Pride thinks he's doing Joy a favor, but Joy is afraid, sad, and confused. How would you describe the impact Mr. Pride has had on Joy's life?

2. How would you describe the impact Joy had on Mr. Pride's life? Mr. Pride assumed Joy is grateful for the things he has done.

3. If Joy could talk what do you think she would tell Mr. Pride about the impact he has had on her life?

**The intent doesn't always match the outcome.**

1. Mr. Pride intended to take good care of Joy. He took her from her family and country, gave her food, a place to live, and a shackle around her ankle. He eventually took the welded chains off of her. When she was too old to work at the circus, he took her back where he found her and dropped her off. Was that a good idea? Explain

## Conversation questions starters for Pride and Joy

- Tell or write your ending to this story and tell why?

- Why was Joy standing in that spot?

- Did Joy have a family?

- Was Joy waiting for Mr. Pride?

- Was Mr. Pride doing a good thing when he took Joy to become part of his circus?

- Do you think Joy was ever happy?

- Is pride a good thing? Explain.

- Do you think the names of the characters were important to the story? Explain.

- What does it mean to be **solely dependent** on someone? Is it a good thing? Explain

- Does being in a hard situation make you a strong or weaker person? Explain.

- Why didn't Joy feel loved or happy?

- Was Mr. Pride taking good care of her?

- What is the moral of this story?

- Rewrite this story with your own ending and share it with others.

- There are **situational opportunities** in every life as when a person finds himself in a position of power like Mr. Pride or a position of oppression as Joy did. What do you think needs to be taken into consideration during times like these?

# The Fishing Trip

## Story #2

It was a perfect day to go fishing. A quick peek out of the bedroom window revealed an overcast sky. Eli could feel the cool bite in the air as it blew in through the window next to his bed. For a short time, Eli watched the squirrels scampering all around and listened to the birds sing. The squirrels seemed to be enjoying a vigorous game of tag as they ran from tree to tree.

Sunrise! It was finally time to get up. Eli jumped out of bed, ran to the bathroom, and quickly splashed a little water on his face. He got dressed, grabbed his things, and was on his way out the door when his dad called him into the kitchen. "Listen, Eli, be careful, remember to leave those freckled and striped worms alone. Don't try to use them for bait. I know they seem harmless, but they aren't. I've heard it said if even one of those worms was used for bait, it would catch the biggest fish in the lake. I think that's more legend than fact because nobody has ever told about it firsthand. So, use the bait I taught you to use. Be back here in three hours, and don't be late!"

This was Eli's first-time fishing alone. His father felt sure he and Eli were ready for this challenge. This was truly a special day for both of them. Eli felt like this talk was taking forever. He could hardly keep himself still long enough to listen to his father's words. But he managed. He could not wait to prove his newfound manhood to his dad. The nod of his father's head was the signal to Eli the conversation was over, and Eli was free to go.

Eli turned and headed for the back door as quick as his feet could carry him. Before he reached the backyard gate, he heard his father's warning, "Remember! Stay away from those weird looking worms, son."

"Okay, Dad," Eli shouted as he continued on his way.

Eli had already walked about half a mile. He could see their favorite fishing spot through the trees ahead. On the way, Eli collected several worms. There were big fat juicy worms, short little wiggly worms, and l-o-n-g skinny slow worms. They were all making their way through the dirt Eli put in the coffee can the night before. Once Eli started fishing, he didn't want to stop. After all he only had three hours in which to catch a lot of fish, get back home, and prove to his dad he was responsible enough to meet this challenge. Eli wanted so badly to impress his dad. Eli's dad had always been there for him, teaching him important lessons about becoming a man, and this was Eli's opportunity to prove he had learned the lessons well.

Eli already knew to stay away from the worms his dad was talking about. His dad really didn't have to tell him again. Eli had heard all the stories about them during fishing trips with family and friends. Eli and his friends did wonder if there was any truth to those stories. From time to time they would use sticks to play with those weird looking freckled and striped worms but not one of his friends ever picked one up with his fingers.

Eli got to thinking about some of those stories as he looked for more bait. Boy, if those worms could really get fish that easily it would be worth it to try just one, he thought. Eli noticed those forbidden worms seemed to be coming out in abundance. It almost seemed as though they wanted to play, but Eli's mind was set. He knew the rules.

As Eli walked further along, he couldn't seem to stop thinking about the forbidden worms. "It sure would be nice to catch the biggest fish in the lake," he said to himself. Eli imagined himself holding up a huge fish. He imagined all his friends gathering around as he told the story of how he landed the big one. If even one of those stories were true, Eli wouldn't need all those other worms. Or so he thought. By now the words of his father seemed to be screaming on the inside of his head. "Son, leave them a-l-o-n-e!" But Eli paid no attention. His focus was already changing from what his dad told him not to do, to what he wished would happen.

Those forbidden worms looked more inviting than ever. Their outward appearance was kind of mesmerizing because their freckles and stripes made different kinds of patterns as they slithered through the dirt together. Eli curiosity got the best of him. He picked up a stick with his left hand and pointed it down until it touched the ground. Sure enough, one of the worms accepted his invitation and crawled up the stick. Eli raised the stick up in order to get a better look. He was now holding the stick with both hands. Then he just watched to see what the worm would do. He watched as the tiny worm inched its way back and forth between his hands. Before Eli realized how close the worm had gotten, it was crawling across his thumb. Eli was stunned. He didn't know what to do, so he just watched some more. Nothing was happening. The worm didn't do anything to him that he could tell. Were those forbidden worms getting a bad reputation for no good reason? Eli did feel something on his hand, but it didn't bother him at all.

Thinking that everyone was wrong about these unusual creatures, Eli decided to use them for bait after all. He emptied the worms he already had in the coffee can and began to fill his coffee can again. But this time he would use the forbidden worms. Eli did notice that every time he picked a worm up, he felt the tiniest little prickle. This surprised him because it didn't hurt, not even a little. By the time Eli got to their favorite fishing spot, his coffee can was full. He couldn't wait to tell his dad how wrong everyone was. Not only would he be able to brag about catching a lot of fish, he would also tell about the harmless forbidden worms firsthand. This was going to be a great day for sure.

By the time Eli finished filling his coffee can the second time he had reached the fishing spot. He baited his hook and began to fish. Eventually a feeling of being cold and a little bit shaky was coming over him, but it was not enough to make him think there was a problem. It was nippy outside. He lowered his hook into the water and before he knew it, he was looking at the biggest fish he had ever seen! Eli was so excited because he thought for sure he was holding the biggest fish in the lake. The weakness he was feeling did puzzle him but not enough to spend time thinking about it. Gathering up his prize-winning fish, the rest of his equipment, and going home was the only thing on his mind. But every step seemed to be harder to take than the last one. Eventually everything felt much heavier. Even standing up was becoming a problem.

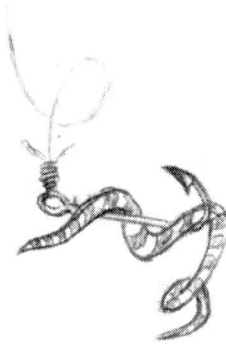

By now Eli was beginning to realize he was in trouble. But what happened he wondered? He started out feeling just fine. "This makes no sense, none at all," Eli managed to say just above a whisper as he recanted his thoughts out loud.

The legend his dad spoke about was coming back to him now. Especially something about catching the biggest fish in the lake because Eli was sure he was carrying it at that very moment. There was a second part to the legend, something about it being more legend than fact, but what did that mean? There was also the part about no one ever passing information on firsthand.

Everything was beginning to make sense. The pieces of this puzzle were coming painfully together, and Eli knew for sure he was in trouble. He realized he had allowed his desire to catch the biggest fish in the lake to play out in his imagination, and it influenced the choice he needed to make next. The good news for Eli was he was so late that his dad was already walking down the path they had walked together so many times before.

# Conversations starters for The Fishing Trip:

1. Was the dad wrong to let Eli go by himself? Explain.

2. Give some clues that tell how Eli and his father felt about each other?

3. If you were the father and everything turned out okay, would you give    Eli a second chance to do it over again?

4. If everything did not turn out okay, whose fault was it? Explain.

5. If you were Eli, would you argue that it is

    A. better to do as your told

    B. trust the people who love you or

    C. do things your own way? Explain.

6. What is personal responsibility and what would it look like in this situation?

7. Is imagination a bad thing? Explain.

8. Is choice a bad thing? Explain.

9. Add a question of your own, and then answer it.

10. After the discussion, rewrite the ending of this story.

As it turns out, those weird looking worms weren't worms at all. They were very small poisonous snakes that just showed up in that area one day. No one ever questioned what they were or where they came from. They just assumed they were worms, and then took each other's word for the rest.

# Abel

## Story #3

Anger and Rage were ready to go on a rampage and any excuse would do. The only thing holding them back was the boy whose body they occupied. His name was Abel. Abel didn't talk much. He grew up in an environment that was unstable, un-predictable, and unforgiving most of the time. He was a teenager now and upset by the slightest things. His emotions went from annoyed to rage in a matter of seconds. It could happen so fast that even Abel would be surprised.

One day Abel arranged to meet up with his new friend Grace. He really liked her. He noticed that when he was with her things didn't bother him so much. He was going to spend time with her this evening, and he was happy about it.

He was walking with quick steps and was almost there when he noticed that someone was following him. Every time he slowed down, that someone slowed down too. He was frustrated by the unwilling dance he and this unidentified stranger seemed to be doing, so he slowed his pace even more. More than anything he wanted to know who this was and what they wanted. Whoever it was would not allow him to get close enough to find out.

He decided to walk faster for at least a block or two to see if he could look back quick enough to get a glimpse of them, so he did. He sped up. The good thing for him was that the sun was just setting, and the streetlights were coming on. Wanting to use this to his advantage, he picked up a little speed, ducked into an alleyway, and peeked back around the corner of a building just in time to see the silhouette of an old acquaintance.

Abel could not believe his eyes. It was Fear! Abel quickly ducked his head back into the dark alleyway and took a deep breath. Breathe easy he thought to himself. He was absolutely shocked because he had already told Fear weeks ago to stay away from him. Fear had caused him to miss out on so many opportunities to make and keep friends and try new things.

His relationship with Fear kept him isolated, and he was sick of it! Fear was linked to so much other stuff like fear of making wrong decisions, fear of being hurt, fear of failure, fear of being alone, panic attacks, fear of embarrassment, humiliation, and more. That's why he told Fear not to come around anymore, and this time he meant it.

He was beginning to realize that every time Anger and Rage acted out, Fear had something to do with it. Fear would be there but go unnoticed. Every time they showed up, they were in control - not him. Sometimes they threw things, broke furniture, or threated people, and each time Abel would promise himself and others that it would never happen again. At one time in his life he thought they were his most dependable protectors. Nobody understood him or wanted to be bothered with him, and he understood why.

Abel had to acknowledge when they were done wreaking havoc and he was back in control he felt a sense of relief and noticed his ability to focus was better. Only by that time, he was too tired and embarrassed to care or stick around. He felt trapped in his ways and wanted help but didn't know what to do about it.

That's where Grace came in. When she was around, life seemed to make a little more sense. She would actually listen to him and how he was feeling. He knew that she was not judgmental but would speak her mind. He felt like she was nice but definitely not a pushover.

He knew if they were going to be friends, he would have to master his emotions, implosive behavior and words. One day Grace was talking to him about something called personal boundaries. He had never heard about it before, but it sounded interesting, and he wanted to know more. Maybe this personal boundary thing could work for him too. For the first time in a long time, Abel was feeling hopeful. Maybe he could be friends with someone and actually leave Fear, Anger, and Rage out of it.

Grace also talked to him about her friend Forgiveness. Abel had definitely heard about her and wanted nothing to do with her. He felt that a relationship with her would cause him to be weak and would be a waste of his time. In order to be friends with her, he would have to let all the people who caused so much chaos, abuse, and abandonment in his life off the hook, and he was not about to do that. Abel did want to be friends with Grace but not so much with her friend Forgiveness, and he had let Grace know exactly how he felt about Forgiveness.

Abel could tell that Fear was following him because whenever Fear was around, his thinking would begin to fog up. For example, even when Abel knew what he wanted to do, so many other thoughts crowded his thinking that he had a hard time staying focused on the particular thought he wanted to process.

In fact, it was happening to him right at that very moment. He was having a hard time remembering where he and Grace agreed to meet. Was it at the Anger Management Grill or Repentance Café? Both places were fairly new in town. Both had been in town for about a year and already had good reputations for their food and service.

Abel had gone to the Anger Management Grill when it first opened and liked it. He did find the atmosphere to be bit challenging because the music was loud, and the people had to talk even louder so their friends could hear what they were saying. The place was packed, and the seating was too close together for his liking, but clearly Anger Management was going to be a booming business. Abel decided he would go there first since it was closest.

His heart was racing now, and to add to his frustration, he had rushed out of the house without his phone. So, calling Grace was not an option.

Abel was beyond annoyed. People usually described his personality as unstable, un-predictable, and unforgiving most of the time. The environment he grew up in eventually became his personally traits.

His longtime friends Anger and Rage were ready to erupt and let the pieces fall where they may, but he was restraining them. He was determined not to let them ruin his night.

The good news was the Anger Management Grill was in sight. Hopefully Grace was already there. He opened the door and walked into a lively atmosphere. At one table the people seemed to be debating something that must have been very important. One person would make a statement, and another would counter it and another person from that same table would chime in to remind everyone that they were there to relax. This was a very busy place, and he was not sure it would be the best atmosphere for them. He walked through looking everywhere. No Grace. He was disappointed and excited at the same time.

The Repentance Café was just a few blocks away, and he was hoping that she would still be there. As he was approaching the café, he could see through the huge decorative window that there were a lot of people inside. He hurried up the three steps that led to the door of the Cafe, opened it, and looked around. He and Grace spotted each other at the same time. He walked right over to where she was sitting and sat down.

"Thanks for waiting," he said.

"No problem. I knew you would get here sooner or later," was her comment.

They both laughed as Abel began to tell Grace everything from what he was thinking to how Fear was following him. He felt that Fear, Anger, and Rage might be powerless in her presence. Abel really wanted this new relationship because he felt that things would be easier to figure out with her around.

Their conversation got very intense when Grace brought up her friend Forgiveness. Abel was doing most of the talking now. When he finished, Grace handed him a menu and suggested that they order something to eat.

"Good idea," he said. They agreed that making a selection was hard because everything on the menu looked great. After a brief discussion, they made their selections, gave their orders to the waitress, and returned to their conversation. Only this time it was Grace's turn to talk.

She explained that her friend was always so misunderstood. She went on to say, "Forgiveness teaches how having boundaries provides the power to let go, disconnect from negative people, places, and things and allows them to move on in a positive state of mind. She also says that people should use the past as research for making informed choices that bring about change."

"What is that supposed to mean?"

"It means to try to understand the problem, identify what you want to do about it, and then bring the wisdom forward, apply it to the best of your ability and leave the trash behind."

"What's the trash?"

"Trash is all the stuff that continually causes your heart, mind, and soul pain and never seems to go away. Forgiveness, also tells people to respect their journey."

"And respect their journey m-e-a-n-s?"

"It means all the life lessons you've learned along the way are important. Use that information to make your life better place."

"Wow! Your friend sure does say a lot of stuff!"

Both of them thought that the way he responded was funny and were having a good laugh as they finished their meal. Things were going well until another customer who was caring a tray with one plate of food and a large soft drink on it bumped into the back of Abel's chair. The tray tipped over, the food fell one way, and the drink went the other way. The icy soft drink cascaded down the back of his head, onto his neck, down his back, and soaked into his shirt. In that short span of time, his reflexes already had him standing on his feet.

Abel finished wiping himself down with napkins about the same time the customer finished getting the mess up off the floor. They were standing face to face.

Abel said, "You owe me an apology."

The customer said, "It was just an accident." And then added, "Get over it!"

Abel was not happy. He felt this customer owed him an apology, accident or not. He had learned from his past not to let anybody (as he saw it) disrespect him like that.

Abel was all reflex and adrenaline now. His longtime defenders were in agreement and ready to pounce. Before Abel realized what was going on, he had grabbed the customer by his shirt and positioned him to receive a punishing blow with one hand awhile at the same time positioning himself to deliver and land that same blow with the other hand. When he was in this state, his strength seemed to increase.

His fist was just about to make contact with the customer's face. He was so out of control that he couldn't hear the other customers yelling for him to stop.

Directly in front of him was the same big picture window he was looking through on his way in. Only this time he was the center of attention. He could see this entire crazy scene as though it was etched into the glass. For a brief second, time stood still, and for the first time he was able to see what other people saw. What made it even worse was that in the very center of this image sat Grace with tears streaming from her face.

**Conversation Starters for Abel:**

1. How can fear go undetected? Explain

2. How did fear, anger, and rage get to be Abel's best friends? Explain

3. Did Abel's friends help him? Explain

4. What happens next, and why was Grace crying? Explain

5. Do you think that Grace was important to the story? Explain

6. What does the word **repent** mean?

7. What did Abel do next? Explain



8. Tell or write the end of this story. What happened and why? Explain


These are the vocabulary words to investigate their definitions together. Make your findings part of the conversation.

**Abel**

**Choices**

**Grace**

**Anger Management**

**Repentance**

**Forgiveness**

**Personal Boundaries**

**Personal Responsibility**

# Gamer – An Element of Fear

## Story #4

Adan and Westly were long-time friends. They loved riding their bikes through the neighborhood so fast that the people they were trying to pass had to hurry up to get out of their way. Both of them enjoyed feeling the wind in their hair and the sun on their faces as they escaped imaginary danger and get to safety.

The scenarios would change but the need to make a quick escape was always the same. Each new adventure was better than the last. The problem was that these friends and been together for so long that their escapades were becoming less and less exciting.

Both of them loved the feeling of uneasiness in their bodies. The kind of uneasiness like when you know something is getting ready to happen but you're not sure what. Adan loved that same feeling and more. Some people would call them daredevils.

They were familiar with every nook and cranny of their neighborhood. They had already investigated all the alleys and knew which streets they were connected to. They even had secret club houses in a few of the vacant lots. If you talked to them, they would tell you that exploring was their thing and danger was their game.

Some of the people in the community started complaining to their parents because their disrespect for others was totally out of control. Sometimes people would trip and fall trying to get out of their way.

The good news was that nothing terrible ever happened and the community members were trying to keep it that way. Sadly, these friends thought these near misses were so funny that they turned it into a game. They called it, "people dogging". The friends enjoyed it, but nobody else did.

Eventually the joy rides slowed down until they came to a complete stop because Adan and Westly had found new ways to feed their need for excitement and fear.

They were no longer happy with temporary feelings of uneasiness that came and went when the fear fun was over. They stumbled upon scarier stuff that was way more fun. The kind of fear they were engaging stayed with you and went with you everywhere. Nether Adan or Westly bargained for what was about to happen.

The new entertainment of choice was screen games. They played every kind of action-adventure board game, video game, fantasy games, and action-adventure virtual reality game they could get their hands on. Wow! What a rush! Some of the games were age appropriate but most weren't. It was easy for them to get just about anything they wanted. Every now and then they would look at each other, laugh and say, "We are so good at what we do," but never really going into any detail.

They really didn't care which of them won. They were just happy to always have each other to hang-out with. They kept track of things like who made it to the next level first, who had the most lives left, who cast the most magic spells successfully, and who was holding the strongest powers.

Adan and Westly would play these game for hours on end, by themselves, and with each other or with the players in the gaming world. Sometimes it would take days just to get to a next level because the players were all so skilled. Adan and Westly liked being in what was called the "game-room". It was a digital location, not a physical location. Players from all over the world could enter and play each other compliments of the man-made, satellites that orbited Earth.

Gamers were signing into digital game-rooms. Some of them all day long. Players could not see each other, but they could hear one another and control the icons (or avatars depending on the type of game being played) that represented them during the game.

Sometimes both Adan and Westly would be so engaged in a game they would literally fall asleep still sitting at their computers or still wearing their virtual reality headset and hand controls.

Sometimes one of the few friends they had from school would invite them to the occasional birthday party or sporting event. They never accepted. Nope, they liked things just the way they were.

It took a while, but Adan and Westly finally admitted that they were no longer able to just stop playing or turn the games off in real-time. For the few minutes they did stop playing in real-time, they would continue playing in their imaginations testing strategies, prioritizing power attacks, and battling icons. But the only way to know if it was all worthwhile for sure was to actually be there, digitally or virtually present.

Not sleeping regularly, being easily agitated, not being able to focus for long, being intermittently happy, sometimes experiencing quick unexpected anger eruptions and other stuff like that became normal for them.

Adan accepted this as his way of life without even realizing it. Adan never looked for anything different. For Adan gaming was all there was.

Westly was getting tired of the gaming life but wasn't sure what to do about it. It had been a long time since he tried making friends in real life. Reaching out to people face to face was awkward and hard for him to do. One day some kids who were laughing together as they walked down the hallway caught his attention. The kids his age were talking with each other, giving friendly pats on the back, laughing, and running races outside. The kids seemed to really like each other. These things were beginning to stand out a lot. Westly wanted relationships like that real-time in real life.

About a year ago, a new gamer who called himself Reggie showed up in the game-room. The game they were playing had lots of magic, fighting, and levels in it. Reggie, who was represented in the game as a book icon introduced himself to Adan and Westly. It became clear very fast that Reggie had skills and would be hard to beat. That was one of the reasons they liked him so much. Sometimes Reggie would talk as they played the game. None of the gamers in the room minded because he seemed to know a lot about a lot of stuff. Reggie was wise enough to know when to talk and when not to. He enjoyed the mental workout that came as a result of playing the game. Adan and Westly never knew when Reggie would be in the game-room or for how long.

For Reggie this game was a temporary break from reality, and he made sure it stayed that way. Westly was beginning to feel like every good thing in his life was in a fight to exist. He even started checking in with himself at times to ask the question, am I pretending or is this real life?

This checking in process went on for about two years before Westly decided that he was going to be brave enough to reach out and try new things and to meet new people. They had reached the twelfth grade. Westly had already been gradually distancing himself from gaming and Adan. Adan had made it perfectly clear that he would leave the gaming world when and only when he had taken on the best of the best gamers and won. It was all about wining, and for him nothing else mattered.

For Westly it was time to part ways. That's what made Reggie's presence in the game room so important. He would make comments on the game as they played. He seemed to be having a great time but when he got tired of it, he would say good-by and disconnect. That was huge to Westly.

Reggie had been playing games like these for years. That's how he understood the draw. At one time he was driven to and by an addiction to gaming. Reggie started playing in third grade. This is one of his accounts that took place. He didn't tell it all at once. The gamers were now entering the digital game-room to play the game and to hear what Reggie had to say.

"My friends and I were into the games," Reggie began. "We had all the cards. We all sat together at the table in the cafeteria. At recess we acted out imaginary scenarios. After school and all weekend, we would be on the computer playing. We would act out our choices using the icon or avatar we had chosen to represent us during the game. At that time, the games were not so sophisticated, but that didn't stop us from being obsessed with them.

We were co-existing in this physical world and an imaginary world of make believe at the very say time. We even had something I call, "video-game-real-time-language." All the words and phrases we used while playing the game on the computer, we used to express real life stuff. Like, 'I died' which meant, 'the game is over.' If I wanted the game to be over because I wanted to be done and try again, instead of just saying that I would say, 'I'm going to commit suicide.' If I was playing a game and lost five points, instead of saying five points I would say, 'I lost five lives.'

If we couldn't play the game on the computer, we would all get out our decks of role play playing cards. If we couldn't have the cards, we would role play the games on the playground. Sometimes players got hurt because they really got into it. If you were the one who hurt someone you, just said the word, 'sorry' and kept on playing. The word, 'sorry' was kind of a free pass. It happened a lot, but one time it got completely out of control, and it changed my life forever.

On that particular day a friend in our group got so carried away that he actually choked the kid who was pretending to be the bad guy. We were supposed to be using the power of the character we were channeling to control and capture each other. Later the kid who did the choking said that he felt like it was real and could not stop himself.

We couldn't get him to let go, so we started yelling for help. A playground staff member who was standing nearby heard us and pulled him off. It freaked us all out. That surprised everybody.

The police had to be called because his hand and finger marks were still on our friend's neck. The boy who did it was really sorry and scared. He couldn't believe what he had done. It seemed like he was in a kind of trance. Then he started crying and shouting something like, 'Why did I do that?' It was hard to make out the words.

After he calmed down, he told staff that he was very confused and did not understand why he became so angry or why he could not remember that he was just playing a game. Everybody knew that in real life he never did stuff like that." Shortly after the story, Reggie said his good-by, disconnected, and left the room.

Everyone in the game-room heard the account. Adan was unfazed. Westly was fully engaged. Reggie's story was right on time because both Adan and Westly had already encountered the same thing. The impulsive unexplainable anger. Only it was directed at family members and sometimes strangers and then afterwards being surprised by their own behavior.

Adan said that if people would leave him alone, things like that would never happen. Westly said that he was feeling out of control and wanted to figure out what to do about it.

The uneasiness and fear they were looking for was present all the time, only this time nobody liked it. Adan decided to accept it because he was still being entertained by it, but he was no longer in charge. It was.

Westly was so tired of it he told fear, right out loud, to get away and stay away from him. Westly said he was even feeling haunted by it. Desperate to make it stop, he disconnected from the game-room, shut down every account, and started looking for advice.

What would you tell him?

**Definition of *virtual reality* - :** an artificial environment which is experienced through sensory stimuli (such as sights and sounds) provided by a computer and in which one's actions partially determine what happens in the environment *also* : the technology used to create or access a virtual reality https://www.merriam-webster.com/dictionary/video%20game

**Definition of *role-play* - 1:** to act out the role of
**2:** to represent in action students were asked to *role-play* the thoughts and feelings of each character— R. G. Lambert https://www.merriam-webster.com/dictionary/video%20game

**Definition of *imaginary* - 1a:** existing only in imagination **:** lacking factual reality - https://www.merriam-webster.com/dictionary/video%20game

**Definition of *image* - 1a:** a visual representation of something - https://www.merriam-webster.com/dictionary/video%20game

**Definition of *hologram* - :** a three-dimensional image reproduced from a pattern of interference produced by a split coherent beam of radiation (such as a laser)*also* : the pattern of interference itself - https://www.merriam-webster.com/dictionary/video%20game

**Definition of *avatar* - 1:** the incarnation of a Hindu deity (such as Vishnu) - **2a:** an incarnation in human form - **b:** an embodiment (as of a concept or philosophy) often in a person - https://www.merriam-webster.com/dictionary/video%20game

**Violence** -*Noun – 1* behavior involving physical force intended to hurt, damage, or kill someone or something. Google.com

# Conversation starters for **Gamer – An Element of Fear:**

1. What is violence? Explain

2. What is roleplay? Explain

3. Does the presence of blood mean that the game is violent?

4. When playing a game using an avatar, which persona (you or it) is making decisions? Explain.

5. The good thing about video, screen, or virtual reality games is…

6. The bad thing about video, screen, or virtual reality games is…

7. Describe the connection between the real life player and imaginary roleplay characters.

8.  What parents need to understand about violence in video, screen, or virtual reality role-playing games is…

9.  Explain why video, screen, and virtual reality games are or are not considered violent.

10. How important is the presence of violence in video games? Explain

11. The words and phrases most commonly used when playing these games are… Make a list. Talk about the meaning, relevance, and impact. Words are very powerful. You can send them out, but you can't take them back. Someone once said you can squeeze the toothpaste out of the tube, but you can't put it back in the tube.

12. How often do you play your favorite game (s) and for how long?

13. How many players are usually playing at one time?

14. Have you ever seen the players in real life? Is this okay? Explain

15. Name ten games, and then number them according to how much you like them.
    a. What is the objective of the game?
    b. List Icons and what they represent?
    c. How many levels?

16. Explain what it means to gain and lose lives.

17. Do video, screen, or virtual reality games cause you to act out violently? Explain

18. Do virtual reality games cause you to make better decisions? Explain

19. Do video, screen, or virtual reality games cause you to be better or worse problem solvers? Explain

20. Are video, screen, or virtual reality games based on real life? Explain

21. Do these role play games help to make the world a better place? Explain

22. Is this world better, worse or unchanged by the influence these games are having on the players? Explain

23. If you could tell every game player anything you wanted to, what would it be? Explain.

Remember, everything you do, think, say, and feel is important. Every action has a reaction, every choice has a consequence, and every intent has an impact.

# Little One

## Story #5

On the inside, she may have felt unloved, unwanted, and lonely. On the outside she was beautiful, graceful, and loving. That's how the enemy of the heart was able to grab her. What she was looking for and wanted was someone to just plain love her in a way that she could grow up and thrive.

Isn't that what every little boy or girl wants? Anyway, he saw her need and her kindness and pounced on them by drawing her into his web of carefully spoken lies. She thought he was real and would treat her well because he said and did the things that the other male role models, at least to this point, wouldn't do for her.

So, he entrapped her in his diabolical plan, and before she realized it, her whole life went up in flames and horror. And she got blamed, and all she really wanted was to be loved by her beloved.

And so, it was.

There was no way for her to know the price she would pay for trying to be one with a man who had no good intent for Little One.

So where was her father? He had decided not to fill the position of father, but he didn't tell her because he wasn't aware that that was what he had done. He didn't know how to properly care for his daughter, Little One. She did love him though, but that's just the way it went.

We don't know the whole story. She was the only one who can tell it. I admire her so much because she was brave, deserving, and strong.

What about Little One's mother? Same thing applies. Her mother was there but didn't know how to be wise about bringing up a daughter because of the relationship she had had with her mother. But her mother absolutely loved her.

Little One's mother, like her father, suffered from broken hearts. When it came to raising their family, they continued in that same generational confusion (like most of us do) that caused every good thing to have to fight just to show up. Were their good days? Yes, for sure! She remembers them.

She had to leave in a hurry. Leaving everything she had and her loved ones behind. It was a hard decision to make but it had to be done.

There was nothing easy about it. One morning Little One got up and went about her day not knowing what was about to take place. She was absolutely surprised! Every demon from hell seemed to have erupted right in front of her eyes. What? She couldn't believe it! Nothing like this was ever supposed to happen! Her mind went into override, and overdrive and stayed there for some years while Little One tried to sort everything out. "How did I get to this place?" Little One thought. "There is truly no way out."

She reached for understanding, direction, and clarity. She had no idea any of this would happen. She was just looking for someone to love and to love her the same way.

Just before her life exploded, she realized that she had to get away. That was her private plan but so…so…. so, many unpredictable events took place, it was raining craziness, and chaos, and, and, and one day, and wait a minute please, she said, "I can never seem to quite catch my breath. I will have to put the pieces together to make sense out of this mess."

The loss was sooooo great. Hearts and relationships broken. So many family members, loved ones, and people at stake. The few people around her who took her in were saying things like "hold on," "don't self-destruct," "let us help you," and "let us guide you until you can walk by yourself."

She was holding several pieces in her hand, and they were still broken and important, and will be placed into the puzzle when it's time to put them in. There is no set deadline as to when.

But for right now, Little One has grown up a lot. She was doing some healing and helping and leading and walking when she noticed that she was able to breathe freely again. And she liked it! People began saying things to her like, "You are beautiful, graceful, loving, and strong."

Little One had finally learned how to believe it. As it pertains to love and being loved back, Little One understands that she deserves to be loved by the right kind of man and expect him to love her back in that same sort of way.

Now she knows that love is patient and love is kind. It does not envy, it does not boast, it is not proud. It does not dishonor others, it is not self-seeking, it is not easily angered, it keeps no record of wrongs. Love does not delight in evil but rejoices with the truth. It always protects, always trusts, always hopes, and always perseveres. And that is exactly what Little One deserves.

So little girl, whose name is Little One, good job on growing up and learning how to love. Put yourself first because your voice is important, and it needs to be heard.

Now tell us about the things you've lived and learned. Share with us your insights and thoughts on how to heal. How to avoid the pit falls and traps that come our way. We need to get the victory over this enemy of our soul, who keeps targeting and, entrapping and, inflicting this unimageable pain.

We don't expect you to know everything just share with us knowledge you have gained. Everyone, please be quiet. Please take your seats. Little One is about to speak.

**Conversation questions starters for Little One:**

1.  How old do you think Little One was when the trouble happened? Explain

2.  How old do you think she was when she began to understand that everything that took place was not her fault? Explain

3.  What do you think it means to have a broken heart? Explain

4.  What does, "raining craziness" mean?

5.  Do you think having a broken heart can be a problem for people? Explain

6. When Little One decided that she was not going to let the chaos control her life, what steps do you think she took? Explain

7. If you could ask Little One a question what would it be? Why?

8. If you could give Little One encouraging words, what would you say?

9. If you had troubling things going on, who might you talk to about it?

10. Don't forget that you too are beautiful, graceful, loving and strong.

# Survivor's Remorse

You are supposed to be here! None of you knew when you went in, who would come back out and who would stay in. It didn't even cross your mind. When the call came, you ran towards the flames. Everyone did their job. Everyone sacrificed, but you were the one who walked away. Then you asked the questions, "Why me? Why did I live and not them?"

You are supposed to be here! When you got the call to go and said, "No, and don't you go either!" You knew the situation had to be handled but not in that way, so you didn't go, but they did. For a minute, things were quiet, and then the phone rang. All hell had broken loose. There was screaming, and crying, and shouting, and you were told to come see. When you arrived, you could not believe your eyes. Reality as you knew it was over. Lives would never be the same. Now you continually ask yourself, "Why didn't I go? What if I had said, 'Yes?' Maybe this tragedy would not have progressed."

Some of the people in the community said you should have gone when called, then blamed you for not being in the midst of that mess, and some of them were your family members too. There was no way for you to know what was going to happen that night. They chose not to listen to you, and you regret not being there and losing them, but do you know for sure that it would have made a difference? Then you asked the question, "Why me? Why am I living and without them?"

You are supposed to be here! You were standing right next them. You could feel the breeze from the bullet's as they flew past your head. Why did you run and leave them behind because leaving was never the plan? There was no plan! You reacted to the loud, disconcerting sounds, and the next thing you knew… How could you have let terror scare you and get you to move? And now you regret it with all of your heart. Then you asked the question, "Why me? Why did I live and not them?"

44

You are supposed to be here! You died in my arms. I had to go. There was nothing left to say or do. I would have gladly traded my life for yours, but that was not an option. Why me and not you?

Why are you still here, you ask? The reason is because we need you. There is something in you that you must share. After all you've been through, after the stinging and repeated dreaming, and wondering why them and not you, please allow the healing. Talk about things that you've been through so when you are finally able to breath, pick the words that best express you. The things that are on your heart. We need to learn from you.

Pleases share your burden and blame, and release the hold that bondage claimed. Because you are loved, and we need you to be just how you are. We need you to choose life, then live.

# Conversation questions starters for Survivor's Remorse

1. If a person survives something, should they have remorse? Explain.

2. What do you think survivor's remorse means?

3. Why do people sometime focus their grief on the survivor? Explain.

4. What are some steps a person who is feeling this way should take?

5. If a person was feeling this way, who would be good helpers for them to talk with?

6. How do you think family, friends, and community help?

Made in the USA
Monee, IL
03 September 2020

39017658R00028